ALEXANDER

House of Otter

Before ALEXANDER

Leo Sparx

4 Horsemen
Publications, Inc.

4 Horsemen Publications, Inc.
1497 Main St. Suite 169
Dunedin, FL 34698
4horsemenpublications.com
info@4horsemenpublications.com

Cover & Typesetting by Battle Goddess Productions
Editor Tilda M. Cooke

E-Book ISBN: 978-1-64450-157-3
Paperback ISBN: 978-1-64450-158-0

Dedication

To the writer's groups,
otterwise none of this would
be possible.

Queer Zoology

Otter (n): *a man who is leaner than a cub or bear but still covered in fur*

BEFORE...

I was naked in a hotel room, somewhere in France, where everything sparkled. The drapes on either side of the long windows were illuminated by an afternoon sun in a city I still hadn't seen, but there was still no sign of the man who had brought me there. On my lap, a shining silver tray sat balanced between my bare legs. In contrast to the dark hair of my thighs, orange slices were stacked on a platter, vibrant as the last sunset I could remember. The one in a little beach town where people called the closest body of water an ocean, but never the sea.

It was brave to have white sheets, I thought, while my lips curved around the flesh of the juicy fruit. Small droplets from my bite landed on the pristine linens, and I rubbed the nearly translucent liquid into the flawless fibers. I didn't know when the man would return, but I didn't want him to determine me ungrateful for everything he'd offered since our trip began.

There were still defined burn lines on my waist and mid-thigh from waking up shirtless only the morning before. In a different place, where I'd spent a starlit night pressed to a flat lounge chair squished into the sand. When the man hung over me in a business suit, silhouetted by the newly risen sun and cloudless teal sky, my body was not yet ready to face the day. In the brief hours before the tourists would arrive to knock down the remnants of forgotten sandcastles, I was half-asleep with my stomach against the stretchy plastic when I pretended not to hear him approaching. From the corner of my eye, the man's charcoal shadow in the warming tan grains said, "Turn over, boy."

Complying to the demands of mysterious men wasn't entirely new to me, but I still hesitated before scooping my sunglasses from the shady area under my chair and slipping them across my eyes. With the saturation of the rays toned down behind the lenses of borrowed glasses, I turned on my side, expecting to see a ranger hat or some indication of law enforcement staring back. But in the sudden clarity, it was easier to decipher the shadow's appearance. His skin and maintained scruff, the tie with the perfect knot near his Adam's apple, and his polished shoes hovering on the sand—this man wasn't a cop; he wasn't even working-class. He was *money*.

Speaking didn't seem necessary before I blinked a few times and continued adjusting to the reality I had awoken in. I completed the rotation to my back to let my chest welcome the sky. Sweat pooled in my chest hair, and I still smelled like warm coconut from the suntan lotion I'd been using in place of soap. It had been the closest thing I'd managed to find since bumming around the beach in this new town, using only what I scavenged from bags the visitors left behind.

The man appeared pleased the instant I moved my body, and I laid with my hands behind my head to let him take in the full view. A fraying white drawstring hung in the pubic hair peeking from the top of my swim trunks, and I could feel him concentrating on the area. Aside from the seagulls calling to dawn and a pelican scoping breakfast from an unusually low tide, no one else heard him ask me to pull down my bathing suit.

Looking past the tops of my feet, beyond the end of the lounge chair, rainbow abalone reflected iridescent as the waves rippled in and out. I still had my hands behind my head while small multi-colored coquinas surfaced with the salty flow before burrowing back into the wet sand and bubbling from their hiding spots. It was how I often felt when a man dug me out of my own safety. When his presence felt like forceful hands trying to remove me from the ground and open my shell. Like I couldn't be beautiful without being bothered.

"Let me see your cock, boy," he repeated. Maybe he hadn't realized that behind my tinted barrier, I hadn't been looking at him. But now, I moved my gaze from the surf back to his jawline.

I pulled my sunglasses down just enough for him to see my eyes. "I'm feeling generous. Are you?" I asked, smirking at his Windsor knot and shiny loafers.

He laughed, unexpectedly bending in his linen dress pants until his knees rested in the sand near my lounge chair. The ocean air made the sweat on my body feel like sea salt ice cream, and when he brought his mouth close to my waistband, I hoped I tasted just as sweet.

"Very generous," he said, using his fingers to toy with the rogue drawstring in the dark forest connected by a single line to my stomach hair. Tracing the pattern north, his hand followed the path up my abdomen until the thick follicles expanded again on my chest. My nipples were starting to get hard, fighting their way through lush curls. Noticing the towers, he brought his index finger and thumb together, circling the perimeter with a light touch before pinching them between his prints.

When my mouth opened to let a quiet moan escape, the stranger seized the opportunity to move his fingers to my tongue. He slid them in and out of my mouth until they were coated with my own slippery spit while he used his other hand to remove my glasses and toss them back into the sand. With his eyes looking into mine, he moved the moisture back to my erect nipples. Immediately, my cock awoke, swelling until it filled the space in my thin trunks.

They were short at the bottom, several inches above my knee and settling at my upper thigh. The man could have easily slid his hand through one of the legs to grip me, but he didn't. Even after moving his attention from my chest and back to the bulge still growing beneath the only fabric on my body, he didn't touch it. Instead, he brought his tongue down to the top of the waistband and tasted the sweat just below my navel. The warmth of his salvia against the chilled breeze made me thicker, but he still avoided the pulsing, now just centimeters from his mouth.

Bracing myself for him to pull me out and devour my length, I was surprised when the warmth of his tongue went missing. He used the metal piping of my chair to push himself up and back in his position above me. Starting at where his fancy shoes found their soles back in the sediment, I watched his shadow again grow tall. The dark image brought his own hand to his lips and sucked my sweat from each of his fingers.

After a final suckling sound, his eyes were on the ocean, not me, when he said, "I believe I instructed you to take out your cock, boy." This was the third time he'd asked. With no further hesitation, I let my thumbs untie the twisted white knot keeping the short trunks around my waist. Whether he paid or not, I wanted to cum, and I wanted him to watch.

Whomever had been the original owner of the bathing suit I'd been wearing, the person who'd selected the fluorescent colors and obtuse triangles from a rack amongst more muted colors and designs, had notable taste. I had noticed, since pulling them from the shade below the boardwalk and bathrooms, that the strange print looked great against my skin.

Perhaps my own sense of fashion had the tendency to sway somewhere toward unique, but it had been quite a while since I'd had the opportunity to choose from anything that hadn't already been left behind or forgotten. Everything I wore these days was retro out of necessity, and I hoped as the man smirked at the sight of my flesh poking through the elastic band, he'd determined my appearance as an appreciation for vintage style instead of an indicator of involuntary poverty.

Out of habit, I flicked at my exposed head before pulling the elastic band farther down my shaft. I could feel his eyes on me still, following the fraying white string until it landed just below my balls and tickled at them. As I grabbed a fist full of my hardness, the man's gaze shifted from my body to something behind me. I craved nothing less than his full admiration and released my cock to turn in the direction he was looking. A blue heron stretched its long beak and legs near a cabana but didn't seem interested in us.

"Haven't seen a heron before?" I asked the man, turning back toward him. His attention returned to me before he spoke. It wasn't the first time I'd seen a tourist impressed by a scavenger.

"We have sea birds in France, just none so..." His words trailed off for a moment while he fixated back on my firm cock dripping with precum in the open air, "large and..." Pressing his lips together and running his tongue across the bottom to moisten them, he finished his thought, "beautiful."

I hadn't noticed his accent before, and I didn't try to stop myself from smirking when I asked plainly, "Why would you vacation here if you live in France?"

The man smiled and broke his gaze with my cock before he walked closer to where I lay on the lounger. He was in my reach again as he bent just far enough down to grab one of the hands I had resting in my pubic hair.

Reaching toward his chest, I was determined to do something sexy; to pull his smooth looking tie until his lips were closer to my body. I didn't get anywhere near my goal before he palmed my other hand and brought them both together so he could hold them both at the wrist.

His grip was firm as he edged his way onto the chair next to me and used a single strong hand to pin my hands above me. With his other, he took hold of my cock and just before pumping at it hard and fast, whispered, "This isn't a vacation, boy."

I wasn't sure if I wanted to ask what he meant, but it didn't matter once he was stroking me from base to tip with my own precum and the briny mist as lubricant. His expert rhythm made the combination of liquids more than enough, and as he pressed my wrists firmly into the plastic ribbons of the lounge chair, all I could see was the intensity in his dark eyes.

The morning dew lingering in the sand filled my senses until I started holding my breath. My head pounded in time with the pulsing of my cock, already prepared to shoot, as my vision and taste disappeared. Everything was replaced with the sound of my own heartbeat and the crashing waves in time with each other, until the man's voice said, "Cum, boy. Give it to me." At his words, for a moment, the world instantly went quiet and dark.

When I opened my eyes again, I saw him staring down and followed his eyeline to the droplets being absorbed into the sediment. I'd always been able to get some distance when I came hard, and it seemed there had been enough power to propel every drip to the sand near my chair. The man appeared both impressed and disappointed.

"I would have liked to have tasted you," he said, releasing my hands and cock to pull a cloth handkerchief from his breast pocket. "Next time, I suppose, boy."

All I wanted to do in that moment was tuck my soft dick into my shorts and fall back to sleep. Maybe find a cabana I could sneak into before the beach rangers began patrolling the area between the surf and shops. The man had drained me so quickly I felt exhausted. He stood back in his original position, and the sun seemed brighter somehow, outlining his frame in a halo of morning light.

Tired and empty as I was, I still expected him to unzip and position his cock for me to exchange the favor. My body fought to stay relaxed, but I prepared myself mentally to get on my knees and suck the stranger to the hilt. Instead, the shadow adjusted his fitted slacks and asked, "Have you been to France, boy?"

My head turned to one side nearly on its own, and I peeked one eye open at him. A smile cracked across my face while I shook my head in response and simply said, "Nope."

He smiled back and laughed a bit, shifting his weight to his heels. "Gather your shirt and shoes, boy," he said. It wasn't a question.

Grabbing my sunglasses from the sand and pushing them flush with my face, I turned back toward the sea to say, "Don't have any."

The tide was higher now, and on any other day, I'd be running down to let the ocean cleanse me before the beach filled with umbrellas, blankets, and french-cut bikinis. It seemed the man had other ideas for my future.

An orange sun ray glistened from a gold ring while he laughed again, scratching his temple with a single finger. I could still see his shadow in the sand, but I didn't want him to know I was paying that much attention. "Well, we've got some shopping to do then," he said, turning his shoes in the grains. He began walking toward the boardwalk and away from me. "Come along, boy."

The tide in front of me continued to wax and wane over the colored shells. Small rainbow clams bubbled for breath from where they had buried themselves. I admired their sense of freedom in a place where most creatures would be drowned or smothered.

Taking a long inhale of salt and young coconut, I turned my head to see the man was halfway through the cattails and up the wooden steps to the boardwalk. He stopped in place and watched me, watching him, with the wind blowing at his suit jacket.

Even in the building humidity, I was frozen for a moment, taking in his full frame for the first time. Like my delay in recognizing his French accent, I somehow hadn't noticed before he was incredibly handsome. With my calmed cock tucked into my shorts, I hung my legs over the chair and let my bare feet touch the crushed shell. Standing between two horizons,

I knew adventure had led me to this town, and now, it was leading me somewhere else.

My expectation was that a man like this one would be staying somewhere with an ocean view. A room with coral colored carpet, turquoise painted walls, and a mirror that made the sitting area look even bigger than it was. Perhaps there would be a kitchenette and a balcony so high nothing could get in aside from the sea breeze. But the trajectory of my fantasy changed as I followed him past the resort buildings to the road where a long black town car waited beyond the small shops lining the boardwalk.

One of the back doors was open, held by a young man wearing white gloves and a chauffeur's hat. He reminded me of a Tom of Finland drawing but less broad in the chest. The moving sketch didn't speak as I tiptoed across the heated pavement but did extend his white-gloved hand toward the interior. I looked back at my host, who straightened his tie as he nodded to the driver. He slid through the door and across the dark leather inside, leaving room for me while I stood paralyzed with gravel between my toes.

"Get in, boy," he said, leaning over to give me a slight smile. Before I could question the possible cons of jumping into a car with a rich stranger, my naked back was sticking to the smooth seat, and the car was rolling over the rocky fragments of the road with light popping sounds.

The windows were so tinted I could hardly see out. There was no way to view our direction through the windshield since it was closed off by a partition between us and the driver. Glass bottles with etched geometric designs glimmered from the sunlight of dawn turned officially to morning, but it was still too early for the stores to be open anywhere in town.

What I wanted was a shopping spree montage in the bustling daybreak of Beachside.

Store-branded bags with braided handles and garments folded by soft hands. I wanted the man to look at my endless reflection in the parallel mirrors of a well-lit boutique and dress me in an ascot or a bowtie like I'd seen in movies, then buy everything I draped over the checkout counter with a satin-finished credit card.

Unintentionally, I was creating a fantasy of him parading me around to his wealthy friends and showing them the scuffed penny he'd found on the beach then buffed to perfection. Even if it was only for a night. Even if that was all he wanted from me.

The duration of our time together was already abnormal compared to the usual quick bangs in semi-private locations. Still, he seemed determined to keep me to himself, or at least away from the people in town seeing us together.

I hadn't been in the beach community long enough to know it well, I just knew the tourists were drawn directly to the ocean upon their arrival. Not only were they forgetful enough from the frozen drinks to leave their belongings behind, but the pressure of having a story to bring back from their vacation to a place where it snowed often meant they were willing to spend ridiculous amounts of money to assure a good time. It was a rare night when I didn't come across a man who had strayed from his family or friends, far enough down the moonlit shore, with a few bucks to spare for a blowjob under the boardwalk.

Even if everything I'd learned about my most recent home had been from the underside of beach showers and public restrooms, I knew enough to sense we were heading west in the town car and had gotten pretty far away from town. When the seagulls stopped cawing and the open sky was replaced with towering greenery, the car stopped in front of a gate covered so entirely with twisted ivy the only legible word was "Otter."

I'd heard the word before, used by men to describe me and men who looked like me. It was the body hair on my compact frame that seemed to be their fascination. That I didn't feel the need or desire to be smooth but wasn't large enough to be considered a bear, or whatever other queer zoology term the community had decided on to differentiate between our body types or fur. Words like that were the language we used to sort each other out but also to make sure everyone was included. Each animal or category was a term of endearment and for some—perhaps like my host—even a fetish, something you could request by name like a cocktail or ripe fruit.

I probably should have been more concerned when the driver forced the gate open and drove through the long stretch to a horseshoe driveway before coming to another full stop in the pebbles. The overgrown vines extended well beyond the first entryway and climbed every inch of the exterior brick. There seemed to be a large wooden door framed by an archway, but it wasn't until the driver opened my door that I was able to get a closer look at the expansive structure.

Something breathed colder on this new side of town where, instead of surf, there were dense trees on either side. The small rocks under my feet almost felt chilled while I craned my neck to take in each story of the house piled on top of the other. It seemed endlessly tall, and by the time I reached the top to visually swallow a single window in a tower, the man spoke, breaking me from drinking the building in.

"Over here, boy." He was holding a long black key and picking the broken plants away as he pushed open the entrance and beckoned me to pass the threshold. I must have hesitated at the blackness which seemed to be lurking on the other side because he checked his expensive watch and tapped at its face with a sigh.

I hadn't realized we were in a hurry, but the bottoms of my feet moved forward on their own at the thought of disappointing him. It was a new feeling for me, caring what a man wanted more than my own comfort. Even a man as rich as he seemed to be had never been enough of a reason for me to respond to commands, but here I was, crossing over the boundary and into the dark house without further question.

With my exposed chest near him, the man slipped by me to press his hand to a wall and flip a switch. Nothing happened.

"Hmm," he said and flicked the switch a few more times. Nothing. "Well, no matter. Up the stairs, boy."

From the light of a morning sun peeking through the door, I could see the general shape of a giant staircase and slowly walked toward it. With my hand stroking the smooth wooden banister, the man followed close behind through lush carpet and art I couldn't make out through the dimness. It seemed strange to me as we climbed higher that despite the opulence of the interior, no one had remembered to pay the electric bill.

"To your right, boy," the man said and pointed toward a hallway lined with closed wooden doors. On either side of the corridor, the furniture lining the walls was covered by off-white sheets. I supposed it was to keep the pieces from getting dusty, but it certainly didn't help with the eerie vibe of the large, and seemingly empty, house.

In this wing with the doors shut and windows covered in the same sheets, the natural light had completely disappeared, but the man continued following close behind. Aside from his occasional directions, the only sound came from boards creaking beneath my steps in time with his rhythmic breath.

When I turned around to look at the man, I heard a sliding sound followed by a thump coming from the end of the hallway. I jumped and stopped where I stood, giving the sound my attention instead of the man. It was difficult to focus my vision on something so far away, but I could make out what seemed to be a sheet on the ground below a painting still hanging on the wall.

Thinking the cover must have slid off the piece of art, I was drawn in that moment directly to the panting. As if it were calling to me. Beckoning me to acknowledge its beauty. I had to know what or who was in the deep-colored portrait. All I could make out aside from the colors was the shape of a figure, next to another that may have been shorter. Maybe an older man in a suit with a younger man sitting next to him—naked.

My feet moved down the hallway without my permission. Toward the two painted men. As I got closer, it was certain, one was seated and the other was kneeling. All I wanted to do was take them in, but in my trance, I felt a furry hand on my bare shoulder. "Back here, boy."

Spinning me back to face a door, he turned the knob and opened it to a massive room. The man had stopped me halfway down the hall, more importantly, halfway from the painting. I could still hear the artful figures calling—something wanted me to reach them—but the man shuffled me over the threshold, clearing his throat and blocking the male voices invading my mind. He closed the door behind us.

Inside, most of the area was filled with a massive bed framed with four posts. This was an orgy bed. A gangbang ring. A circle-jerk pillow fight battleground. But the mattress, like almost everything I'd seen in the house so far, was covered with the same sheeting as though it had been decades since it had been used.

Light from a single window illuminated a giant wardrobe on the opposite wall, and the man, completely ignoring the perfect setting for group sex only a few feet away, opened the hinged doors to reveal hanging clothes. Below were drawers that he pulled open one at a time to rummage through garments. I couldn't see them from where I stood, but he turned with an armful of options. "Take off your clothes, boy."

I assumed he was referring to the bathing suit. We both knew I wasn't wearing anything else unless the sunglasses I'd pushed up to rest in my shaggy hair counted as more than an accessory.

There wasn't much hesitation on my end to pull the elastic band down. It wasn't just because he had already seen the goods. Truth was, if I could be naked all the time, I would be. Given the universal okay to just be dick-out with as little on as possible, I'd go for it. Already I had gone at least a year without even a pair of designated flip-flops. What I'd learned in that time was: people put way too much thought into what they wear in hopes people will ask them to remove it.

So here I was, ratty drawstring around my ankles, my hairy ass not far from a king-sized bed already covered and protected from potential bodily fluids. If he wanted to, he could have bent me over right there. I could have put my back flat on the sheet and put my legs in the air.

No money had been exchanged, but the feeling was the same as any other time I'd been purchased. Or more so my time and my body. But unlike other men, instead of taking advantage of his new action figure's moving parts, he seemed more interested in dressing me. He handed me a jockstrap with a colorful band, then another, and another. He asked me to try on each and spin around until he found the color he liked best on my skin.

"That's the one, boy," he finally said, smirking each time he got a view of my furry ass. I could see he was hard under his slacks before he threw a pair of jeans, t-shirt, and set of boots on the bed near me. They all bounced against the mattress, and I thought about what it would be like to be under him in the spot the clothes landed when he said, "These look like they were made for you."

He seemed pleased enough, but while he was closing the wardrobe drawers, I heard whispers coming through the door. I couldn't be sure if it was the older or younger man in the picture, but one of them told me I wasn't trying hard enough. They spoke in strange words I couldn't understand as more than a feeling, but the sensation of their expectations running through me brought me to my knees in front of the door.

When the man turned around, I ran a hand through my hair to remove the glasses from where they sat perched in my beachy hair then threw them to the side. I spread my legs on the carpet to make sure he could get a full view of my package resting in the new underwear and opened my mouth, wide and inviting. Looking into his eyes as he stepped closer, I swirled my tongue toward the zipper of his pants. His hand was on my shoulder again, and for a moment, I thought I had him.

With a smile, he looked down at me and stroked my tongue with two fingers. I closed my lips around them and sucked as he thrust them deeper inside. He smirked, then sighed, catching a glimpse of his watch not far from my mouth. "We do not have the time, boy," he said, dragging his salty fingertips across my bottom lips as they exited the wet hole. Grabbing the door knob behind me, he motioned to the clothes still sitting on the bed, instructing me nonverbally to get dressed. He made his way to the hallway, leaving me on my knees, hard and waiting.

A sense of disappointment lingered as I waited for my firmness to subside before attempting to close the fly of the tight jeans.

It felt strange, as if the house were communicating with me. As if I had a connection with it somehow. But for the moment, it was quiet. Possibly angry. The real life man was getting what he wanted, but the ones in the portrait seemed to want more than I was able to deliver. Maybe I just needed to eat something.

Convincing myself a real breakfast would clear my head, I finished dressing and carried the boots into the hall. I wished I could have explored the room more; there seemed to be an expansive bathroom with just the corner of a purple bathtub peeking through. A shower, bath, even just a quick splash of water would have been nice. But instead of letting me use the amenities of the massive house, the man tapped at his watch just outside the door. "Hurry up, boy."

Back in the hallway, cobwebs I hadn't noticed before were gathered in nearly every corner and around devices that looked like old speakers all wired together. The man was already down the stairs ahead of me, but when he reached the final landing, he stared up, waiting.

When my foot hit the first step, I couldn't help but swing my head back toward the portrait at the end of the hallway. The men in the painting didn't move or speak, but something told me it wouldn't be the last time I'd see them.

The man stopped in the doorway between the interior and front stoop where the car waited to take us away to wherever we were going. When I stood across from him on the threshold, he smiled and brushed a piece of hair from my cheek. Passion rose hot and electric within me. I wanted to kiss him. He leaned in close for a moment but stopped, as if he had heard something or someone speaking, then pulled away.

"Let's go, boy," he said, motioning for us to move to the town car. "This place never feels quite right this time of the year. Too many ghosts."

International first-class seemed to mean food and wine. It meant hot towels and other things to keep passengers comfortable for a ten hour direct flight. And I was comfortable, letting the plushness of the seat cradle the parts of me still packed with sand. Part of me was still wishing I would have checked to see whether the creepy mansion had running water for a shower while we rode to the airport. But just after take-off, when the man asked me if I preferred red or white blends, the empty manor felt just as far away as the surf, and mattered even less.

Now I was three glasses in and still unsure which one he'd ordered. I'd gotten too used to the last sips of pina coladas and strawberry daiquiris to remember what decent alcohol tasted like. I was surprised how little I missed the miniature plastic swords speared with half-eaten garnishes, water-logged in the bottom like sunken treasure, now that I had clean glass in front of me. It wasn't that I needed to drink to feel relaxed, but the more the long-stemmed goblets piled up on the tray table, the more I felt myself leaning into his seat. Through it all, one thought dominated my mind, I needed to find my way close to his lips again.

"So, what's your name?" I asked. The sound of my own voice made me purse my lips as I swayed toward him. I was definitely intoxicated.

He laughed just slightly but didn't respond right away. Instead, he reached into a piece of luggage under his seat and pulled out a plum-colored bag with a golden pull-string. Something tall and firm was inside, and he grasped it with both hands.

"Oh my boy." The man put his palm on my leg and gave it a light squeeze. "My name all depends on what happens after this plane lands."

I didn't understand what he meant, but now my focus was on the bag sitting between his legs. It was big enough to hold a bottle of liquor. Maybe he was doing his best to get me drunker than airplane wine would allow.

If he wanted to get me intoxicated enough to put my head in his lap and blow him on the plane, I was surprised he hadn't realized, I was already there. So much of me wanted to pull up the armrest between us and slip my jeans down far enough to slide him inside of me. If the flight attendants in their buttons and collars saw us, I just hoped they would watch.

The last drops of my fourth glass down, he handed me the small bag. I tried to untie the golden string at my seat, but he stopped me. With his hands on mine, he pointed to the bathroom at the front of the plane. "Bring the bag back empty. Don't come out until you've taken it all, boy."

A voice with a thicker French accent than the man had, came over the speakers above us. Despite the static overlay, I could make out that he was saying we were halfway through our trip. There were five hours left until I'd see Europe for the first time, which meant five hours to drink whatever was in this bottle and try not to get alcohol poisoning. That, I figured, would be less than sexy. But if I couldn't have his cock or mouth, I would do my best to please him in any way he asked.

In the tight space of the restroom, I balanced the bag on the counter near the sink and pulled the cinched seal wide until it was fully open. The contents emerged slowly through the ruffled hole. Unlike my expectations, the item wasn't clear or filled with liquid. It wasn't a bottle at all. The inner contents of the mysterious bag was black, solid, and shaped like a tree with a rounded point. Pulling the fabric farther down showed a diameter at the base wider than my own fist. Near the bottom, loose in the bag, was a sample-size packet of lube. This was the biggest butt plug I had ever seen.

I was wishing now he had ordered whiskey instead of wine as I transported the silicone plug to the floor and began unzipping my jeans. Something about whiskey always made me feel bold and ready for a challenge. Luckily, wine at least made me want to get fucked. So, with my ass hovering over the bulbous toy in the jockstrap he'd picked out for me, I tore open the lube pellet with my teeth and lowered down slowly. Bouncing on the slippery tapered shape,

I felt my hole open up as I thought about what the man wanted from me.

We hadn't talked about his expectations, or payment, but already I'd gotten a ride in a fancy car, new clothes, and a trip across the ocean. Well, midway so far, at least. In either case, it wasn't terrible for a day I had originally planned to just wake up on the beach and see what I could live off.

Not having a building to call home had become a sort of freedom I learned to enjoy. Wandering into that town, the stars became my blanket and the sand my pillow. But I never planned to stay anywhere forever, and there was no saying where I could wake up tomorrow if I could make the man waiting for me in first class keep smiling.

The squishy pill of lube was bone-dry by the time my hole threatened to stretch over the widest part of the toy. My cock dripped, soaking the jockstrap, but I didn't touch it. I knew if I came it would only make it more difficult to fit the remainder of the firm polyurethane inside of me. It was so big I had to rise again and even thought about giving up. He expected me to bring the bag back empty though, and considering the size of the plug, there was nowhere to hide it on my person. Cher-forbid I stashed it behind the airplane toilet or left it in the bathroom for some poor passenger to find. Either way, I had a feeling he'd know right away if I hadn't complied with his demands, and as far as I could tell, I was on the clock.

I tried again and felt pleased when I got myself pretty far down, but a knock on the door made me stop my momentum. "Just a minute," I said, hands on my thighs, holding my breath with my ass partially swallowing the tapered shape.

"Having trouble in there, boy?" the man asked from the other side of the door. I didn't answer but brought my hands to my knees to boost myself farther onto my feet. My hole tightened instantly knowing he was waiting for me, and before I could answer him, the handle jiggled and the door opened. He stood in the tight space with me, looming again as he had on the beach, standing over me and demanding my sex. He closed the door behind him and pierced with me with an authoritative glare. "All of it, boy," he said.

His words were the motivation I needed to let the rounded tip open my hole again and make me push down. Closer to my body now, his hands on my shoulders from behind pressed just enough.

"Breathe deep, then exhale, boy," he said, reaching down to circle one of my nipples.

I did as I was told, with my hole resting just before the thickest part of the plug. If I could get past it, I knew the thinner part would sit more comfortably. With a deep breath, I felt him rub my chest, and on the long exhale, he pushed down with more force. Enough so the toy thrust its way fully inside.

"There we go. Good job, boy," he said, moving his fingers to where my mouth was wide open and panting.

I felt full, wishing it was his cock but pleased I had proven I could take something so big. Reaching back, all I wanted to do was feel if he was hard, to stroke him in my hand or feel him pushing his length against the back of my throat while I sat on the toy.

But as soon as my hand grazed his dress pants, he again pulled away. He shut the door behind him, and I heard the lock click back in position.

Pulling my jeans over the devoured plug, when I returned to my seat, I could feel everything as I sat down next to him. If I was going to spend five whole hours with this toy inside of me, I hoped that when we landed, I could entice him enough with my open hole to earn his cock.

He had the window seat, but I leaned over enough to see the ocean in what was left of the daylight. It looked different from this height, the colorful shells and shiny creatures smaller than ever.

"I hope you're enjoying my plane, boy," he said and slid the plastic covering on the window closed.

The still nameless man and I were met by a new driver and long black car as the first burst of air of the new climate hit my face. I kept the plug inside of me, but he hadn't mentioned it again since forcing it inside of me in the airplane bathroom. This fresh chauffeur, in his white gloves and Tom of Finland hat, made me wonder if he noticed the precum moistening the front of my jeans as I slid into the backseat. With the toy pushing deeper from the multiple transitions of walking to sitting, if he saw I'd been dripping for almost six hours now, he didn't say anything.

While I sat next to the man in the backseat against new smooth vinyl, the driver looked into the rearview mirror and said, "I hope your trip to the winter estate was satisfactory, Mr. Usher."

The man, Usher, nodded in response, and eyeing me while I wiggled in my seat to adjust the large plug spreading my hole said, "Better than expected," then smiled, just slightly.

We hadn't been driving long when Usher pushed a button on his armrest to raise the partition between us and the driver. "Are you ready to take that toy out, boy?" he asked as the seal closed.

I nodded and felt an unintentional whimper escape me, ready to finally replace the bulbous cone with his cock. He flipped me over and pulled down my jeans, revealing my bare ass framed by the elastic bands of the jockstrap. Pulling at each of the stretchy straps below my cheeks, he let them snap at my upper thighs until the spots began to sting. Then he traced the base of the plug and pushed his finger around my opening until he could force his way past the toy to spread me even more.

Begging for sex had never quite been my style, but I had also never been so completely open. Usher was drawing physical sensations and feelings from me I didn't know existed, a need for his touch and sex. But as I moved my body with the intention of getting his cock near my mouth, he pushed me down. With my face flush to the slick interior, he pulled hard on the toy, attempting to remove it. "Time to give this back, boy," he said as my ass sucked the silicone back in. The resistance felt like quicksand; the harder he pulled, the more my ass swallowed it back up.

When his first few attempts failed, he released for just a moment. "Such a greedy boy," he said and slapped the base of the plug with his flat hand. My cock was dripping again at the sudden impact.

With his other hand still pressing my front-half down, he continued to slap until the skin of either side of my ass burned. Between the snapping of the elastic jockstrap and my cheeks around the toy, I knew my whole back-side was red.

I winced at each strike but tried not to whine or whimper under his force. My cock was so hard from the spanking it pushed against his leg. I assumed he could feel it but knew for sure when he asked, "Does it turn you on knowing you already belong to me, boy? That cock, these holes, all of you is mine now."

And while my mouth said "Yes!" without thinking, my body relaxed, and with a swift tug, Usher removed the giant toy from my body. My hole felt wide and exposed to the air. The feeling made me wonder if the windows were as tinted as the other car had been, or if the people on the highways of France could see straight inside of me. His fingers traced my opening again and I felt something warm inside me accompanied by the smacking of Usher's lips. "Swallow that spit up, boy," he said. The warmth dripped deeper in my hole. I had never wanted a man so badly in my life.

When I felt his force release from my neck and back, I used the opportunity to roll until I could get to my feet and straddle him. The movement must have caught him off guard because he allowed me to get far enough to where I could hover my prepared hole over his cock. I grabbed his hands and put them under my shirt, letting him stroke my stomach and chest while I reached down to unbutton his pants. I knew if I could get to his cock and release it, I could have him in me instantly with no resistance from my body.

Usher grabbed me around the hip and gripped hard while his other hand fought me away from his zipper. He hurriedly whispered, "No boy. We can't." But I wasn't listening. I wasn't paying attention to his commands. Not now, with my cock dripping and hole ready to ride him. I had his button open and zipper half down as he gasped and breathed into my ear, trying to resist me but failing.

It was then the car abruptly braked, and I was flung face first into the back of the seat in front of me. Cock-out and full of spit on the floor of the town car's shag carpeting. How embarrassing. Usher refastened his pants and didn't help me up from the floor before jumping out of the car. He yelled back at me, "Don't move, boy!" before slamming the door behind him. I could barely see from where I laid in the space picking carpet fibers where they stuck to the lubrication on my skin, but I could hear yelling and sense the glow of fire.

I didn't move, but even if I had pulled my jeans back up to sit into the luxurious bench seats—the ones that totally would have had enough room for us to comfortably fuck on—Usher was quickly back in the car, and were speeding off in a hurry. The partition rolled back down and the driver spoke quickly as Usher ran his hands through his own hair and exhaled nervously. "The hotel?" asked the driver, and Usher nodded with fear in his eyes.

The showers on the boardwalk were always cold, and more often I'd chosen the lukewarm salt water to bathe in when given the option. But in the hotel room, the mirrors were steaming from the heat of the large tub I'd filled over and over. Submerged up to my neck, I wished Usher had stayed with me. That I had been given another opportunity to try to fuck him. Maybe in this jacuzzi tub with built-in jets that was surrounded by mirrors. This was the way to have freaky sex, hands down. Being able to see all the dirty things you do to someone or they do to you reflected back into infinity...this was peak luxury.

Unfortunately, I was alone with the sex tub and had an entire suite full of tufted furniture to myself. The man whose name I had learned only hours before dropped me at the lobby with a key and no further instructions aside from, "To the penthouse, boy. Stay there." He and the driver took off once both of my feet hit the pavement in front of the glass doors. I could only assume they were heading back toward whatever danger and chaos we'd driven away from.

I probably should have been more concerned about what I had gotten myself into, but I was in fucking France with a key to a top-floor hotel room next to people in an elevator who only spoke French and tilted their heads at me when I pushed the "P" button on the lit panel. One man looked down at my jeans, at the wet spot, and shook his head. But I smiled back and nodded to them as they exited to their rooms, all lower than my destination. For once, I was the tourist, and I was enjoying every second of making my vacation memorable.

After cleaning every grain of Beachside from my body in the oversized basin, I ate cheese from a rolling cart that was delivered to the room without my asking. When the bellhop lifted the lid of the silver tray, he said, "*Fromage*." So I smiled and said back, "*Fromage*," as if I were saying "yes" or "thank you."

I wasn't certain if the word meant either of the pleasantries I hoped it did, but if he was asking for a tip, I couldn't offer him money. My pockets, although now in a real pair of pants, were still empty. He was cute enough though that if this had been only yesterday, I would have at least offered to blow him through the opening of his tight white uniform. But I didn't.

The bellhop smirked at my terrible French and lowered the top of the tray to the wrinkle-free tablecloth. For a moment, we hung there while he looked me up and down in my robe and moved around the cart to the bed where I was perched. It was nice that French hotels let their staff keep their facial hair, I thought, as he brought his scruffy face closer to mine. I could see he was hard under his thin pants, and my cock was threatening to poke its way through one side of the robe where it split at my legs. Our eyes met and the bellhop wet his lips.

When I pushed him away, it wasn't because my body didn't want him. The motion felt instinctual. As though my lust had a particular craving and an awareness I would not be satiated by just any man. The bellhop pulled back politely and adjusted himself in his uniform. "Hmm," he said, pursing his lips.

He followed the sound with words I didn't understand then nodded and smiled at me before exiting the room. Seeing the shape of his ass before he closed the door behind him summoned an unfamiliar feeling. It may have been regret, but more so it was longing. A deep want for the man who had presented me with such extravagance to return. Alone again with only a plate of cheese for my growing appetite, I could only think about Usher.

One thing was certain: it was easier to sleep in the comfort of a plush bed instead of a metal lounge chair. Even if my ceiling was no longer a starlit sky, I could still see the constellations from the large window of the room. The Big Dipper, the Little Dipper—I'd never been much of a size queen and was always happy to see them both on any night.

Taking them in, something felt the same, but the comfort around me was remarkably different. It was funny now, in a way, to think a sandy shore had ever felt like home. That word, home, had meant so many different places over the recent years, but now, I wondered if this new city could become just that. Of course, I'd have a lot more to learn than just the customs of cruising to get by. I'd need to absorb an entire language and discover just how I could meet the expectations of Usher to not only please, but keep him.

I filled the evening by throwing myself around the expansive penthouse. Rummaging through whatever I could find to entertain myself in the solitude until I fell asleep with a large pillow cradling behind me, imagining it was the man pushing into my lower back and ass. In my half-sleeping fantasy, he was keeping me warm and filling me, teaching me new words that all meant sexy things in French. Whispering "boy" at the end of each of his sentences in my ear and telling me all my cum belonged to him until I realized his presence was a dream and had to shift my naked body so my hardness would stop pushing into the mattress.

When I woke in the morning, I was still alone. The same trays materialized at the side of the bed, but this time with fresh bread and orange slices. There was no sign of the attractive bellhop from the night before, and although it seemed I had slept through his presence this time, I thought about what I would have done if he had tried to fuck me again. If I would have had the strength to keep waiting for the man to appear with sexy food dangling in front of me and my appetite turning quickly to starvation.

Figuring the best I could do with my free time was prepare myself for him, I put on the jockstrap he'd selected for me and sprawled across the bed, arching my back anytime I heard the elevator ding. I wanted the first thing the man saw when he reached the room to be my ass in the air waiting for him. But for what felt like hours, I just lay there exposed and rubbing my hardness against the bedsheets, listening for the high-pitched sound.

There weren't other rooms on the floor; the suite took up the entire top portion of the tall building. So when I finally heard the ding, I adjusted the bands of the jockstrap and arched like hell to make sure my ass looked perfect for him. I used the core-strength I had to keep myself in position, holding my breath, then… nothing.

The knob didn't turn and no one came inside. I listened again, wondering if I had imagined the elevator opening onto the floor. There were footsteps shuffling outside.

Even if it was the bellhop coming to deliver me an early lunch, I didn't know why he was lingering outside the entrance. If it was the man, Usher, maybe he was getting himself ready, stroking his cock through the opening in his pants to make himself firm enough to plunge straight into my hole as soon as he saw me. That would be the ideal scenario.

I didn't release my pose, instead closing my eyes and letting the fantasy take me. I'd been avoiding my cock, but now I stroked it lightly. I wanted him to know I was ready for him. Touching the pulsing I'd been saving for him felt so incredible. I felt like I could cum right away and may have had to actively stop myself if my pumping hadn't been interrupted by a knock.

The door creaked open before I could move from my position. "It's time to go," the voice said. It was familiar, but I couldn't place it right away. I just knew it wasn't Usher.

I turned to see the driver who had picked us up at the airport, the man who had probably seen or at least heard Usher filling my gaping ass with his spit in the back of the car. He slid his gloved hand over the frame of the door while I pulled my legs close to my chest on the bed. My cock was still hard and not getting any softer when I took notice of his body.

My robe wasn't far from where he stood, and when he noticed it, he tossed it in my direction, covering my face for just a moment before I slid it down and draped it over myself.

"You better put some real clothes on before you get us both in trouble," he said and winked.

I hadn't observed before that not only were we around the same age, but like me, he had trimmed facial hair that connected his mustache and beard around his lips. Perhaps if I hadn't been so fascinated with Usher or had a massive toy expanding my ass, I may have taken the driver in when he'd first picked us up. Maybe I would have noticed the incredibly handsome bearded young man hiding under the shiny black hat and wondered what was underneath his uniform.

As he stood in the doorway smiling at me, I thought about picking up the nearby phone. I thought about calling the hot bellhop for a special request to have both him and the driver pound me into the soft linens currently cradling my bare ass cheeks. It seemed like such a waste for them to have just been slept in and not left in total disarray. The three of us could leave them a nice sticky, sweaty mess. That was the kind of room service I deserved in a place like this.

But somehow, a voice pushed through my dirty thoughts. One that I hadn't heard since the day before in the mansion near the beach. It was the voice from the portrait, and it whispered softly but directly. It told me if I really wanted to be financially satisfied, I would save myself for Usher.

In the car, I could only see the back of the young driver's head, his dark hair sticking out from under his hat, when he said in slightly broken English, "It's usually much prettier here." He was commenting on the trees lining the asphalt stretch we were driving on. They were shades of black and grey and appeared charred as though they had been burned.

His English wasn't bad, better than my French by far, and I was happy to have someone to talk to since the bellboy and I hadn't exchanged many words.

"Was there a fire?" I asked, seeing that we were approaching a gate similar to the one in Beachside. The driver nodded before stopping the car just before the gate.

"Some people in town, they…think we are wrong. You understand," he said and opened his car door. From the back window, I could see the metal barrier required a key to unlock a large padlock attached to thick chains woven through the iron bars. On either side was a long brick wall that went on endlessly in either direction until it disappeared into dense forest. When we drove through the gate, the driver exited again to close it all behind him and stashed the key in his coat pocket.

In a way, I did understand. People thinking I was "wrong," as the handsome driver described it, was the reason I left the place where I was raised. Not the beach town, but before that in a life when I was chased from my own warm bed for admitting who I was to people who said they loved me. That moment was the start of a long series of moves and searching for a new place to lay my head. And as the mansion came into view on the other end of the long driveway, I noticed how much it matched the Beachside manor, just larger in scale, and I wondered if I could ever call a place so large home.

Arriving at the house, it looked nearly identical to the one he'd shown me across the sea but somehow alive. One difference I noticed immediately as we walked through the front door was the lights worked, but even if they hadn't, there were enough candles lit to illuminate the vast foyer.

Music was coming from a room just beyond the entrance, and a boy in a jockstrap was delicately playing the violin. Other boys sat listening, all in their underwear with their furry chests exposed. But the first eyes that met mine didn't come from any of them. Instead, it was the familiar pair from the portrait in the other house staring back at me. The same picture and set of men, just silent.

The driver took off his hat and caught me inspecting the painting. One of the men, the younger one, was kneeling and something in his face seemed so familiar. "Who is that?" I asked the young handsome driver. In response, he nodded toward the gay concert hall only a few feet from us and put a finger to his lips. "Shh," he said.

I tried to be polite and listen as he led me closer to the candlelit room full of cushy sitting pillows and hairy crossed legs. When the boy stopped playing whatever melodramatic classical piece he had committed to memory, the young men clapped. I saw a boy eye me then whisper into the ear of the handsome driver. Now stripped down to his own backless underwear and nothing else. As if addressing the entire room, the driver said, "Yes, the American."

Whispers in French were all around me accompanied by mischievous smiles. I was the only one still in my clothes, and soon I was surrounded by the young hairy French men. One pulled at my shirt while the others undid my jeans. Hands covered my body until I stood in just my jockstrap like the rest of them.

It was difficult not to notice the similarities in our bodies. We were all different shades of skin, hair, and eyes, but our frames and the body hair from our faces to stomachs were all the same. Otters. Furry young otters.

One boy spoke. It was all French, but his inflection indicated he was asking me a question. And to his inquiry, I responded with the only French word I'd heard: "*Fromage.*"

All the boys laughed around me until a voice said, "I taught him that." It was the bellboy from the hotel who somehow looked even sexier out of uniform. He walked closer and pinched at my nipple. "That's your name now, you know. You are *Fromage.*"

I couldn't tell if he was flirting or making fun of me, but it didn't matter when I saw all the boys turn their attention to some place beyond me. A voice boomed as it descended closer to us. "No, his name is boy, like all of you." It was

Usher coming down a marble staircase and into the grand foyer, smiling. Near him, standing but attached to a leash by a thick collar, was the other driver. The one from Beachside, before we got on the plane.

Neither spoke while they approached. The room fell silent. But in the candlelight with shirtless men all around me, I didn't feel out of place. I counted the boys where we stood. Including the two drivers, the bellhop, myself, and three more boys I only knew so far by the colors of the underwear—Blue, Green, and a sort of Burgundy—there were seven of us.

As Usher made his entrance, he did little but nod and set a large black whip in the center of the room. The boys seemed well-trained and immediately grabbed colored ropes from a nearby wall. Each boy put his hands behind his back with their rope, and one at a time, they fastened each other in place. The driver from Beachside, still in his collar, approached me with a vibrant orange coil, and without a word, I turned and let him secure me tightly. My cock was rock hard feeling him pull at the cord until he knew I couldn't escape without assistance.

When only one boy remained, the driver in the collar, Usher tied his hands himself and released him into the circle we'd all formed instinctively. We rounded Usher in the dim light and he pulled each boy's underwear to his ankles until all of our cocks were out. The mood was quiet and sinister with the whip sitting in the middle of the polished tile like a threat, and at the sight of my instant firmness, Usher shook his head with disapproval.

I was participating in a game I didn't know the rules to, but as I watched Usher jerk off each boy with spit from his own mouth, I saw them try to fight against the pleasure. They stood in their place and shifted the weight between their feet. They bit at their lips. When they seemed close, he would stop and move onto the next boy, stroking long enough to torment and edge them before taking on the next.

As my turn came around again, I did my best to use their tactics and resist getting excited, but feeling the ropes against my wrist reminded me of when he'd restrained me on the beach. It made me think about how good it felt when he'd jerked me off and opened my hole on the plane. I'd been waiting so long to feel him touch me again, and now, he finally was.

I knew my cock was dripping and watched as Usher tasted my precum and smiled. He whispered, "You're doing well, boy. Just relax," before walking back to the center of the circle to retrieve the whip.

Immediately, the other boys turned their bare asses to their master. They knew the rules, but what they were competing for, I wasn't certain. Usher cracked the long strip against the first boy's hairy nakedness until he glowed on each cheek. I hadn't turned around yet, but when he pierced me with his eyes, I knew I would pay for disobeying him. I flipped my eyes to the wall and offered him my ass, no longer framed by the orange jockstrap he'd selected with intention days before.

I had wanted this then, to have him see my ass prepared and ready for him, but I hadn't imagined it would be like this—with other boys around and sharing his attention. Without warning, the whip thundered against my skin, and each bolt made me consider the reality I found myself in. Around me were endlessly opulent things. A life I could have never had on my own.

A voice whispered, "It can be yours," and I wanted to look at the painting to see if the men in the portrait were speaking to me, but I was afraid to look anywhere aside from the wall while he snapped the tail at my skin over and over.

The pain came over me like a rolling tide, and for a moment, my mind was clear. Usher had come to Beachside for only one reason: to find me and bring me back here. It had been the house that commanded him to include me in this ritual. Not only did I belong in this castle, I had been summoned here. But I still didn't understand why he had left me in the hotel room for so long.

After I had successfully endured the pain Usher dealt, he seemed tired of controlling the whip and commanded that the boys turn back around. He went back to working their cocks until Blue came, then Green, then the bellhop.

It wasn't pleasant anymore, having him stroke me while I tried to hold the cum inside; it was torture. Something told me if I could just endure it a little longer, I would win Usher's love. If I could outlast the rest of the boys, I could have him all to myself.

Burgundy's cock was the type that pointed toward his belly button, and when he exploded, it dripped down the fur on his stomach. Next was the French chauffeur, who moaned and squirmed in Usher's hand before shooting his load so far it landed halfway to where I stood across from him.

Between the American driver and myself, we were the last, and Usher unexpectedly stopped his stroking and pumping. He untied our hands and pulled us each to the center of the circle by our cocks. The boys still tied and surrounding us watched as Usher moved the driver's hand to my cock and mine to his. This was the last round of the competition it seemed, and it was about to be brutal.

Gripping hard and stroking, I didn't know his background, but I'd had years of practice and was confident in my skills. I flicked at the underside of his foreskin and rubbed his own precum up and down his shaft. When I took some of my own to mix them together, I could feel his arousal reaching a peak. His eyes got wide, like he knew he'd already lost. And despite how good it felt to feel his hand around me, when his warm cum dripped down my closed fist, I knew I had won.

Usher smiled at me, and the boys cheered, jumping in place with their jockstraps still around their ankles. It looked like the master of the house was about to announce something, but in that moment, banging came from the exterior of the mansion. Yellow and red light filled the windows and heat soon followed. Something exploded. Then something else. And soon we were all on the ground showered by broken stained glass and fire.

A mob of what must have been people from the town, the ones the French driver had told me thought men like us were wrong, pushed through the front doors. Just before they surrounded us all, I saw the fear back in Usher's eyes as he yelled, "Run, boy!"

On my feet, I bolted for the other boys and tried to untie them. We jumped over cum and whips and toys, dodging the townspeople who infiltrated our sanctuary. I led the boys up the stairs of the house, but every time I turned back, another boy was missing. It wasn't until I grabbed a door knob on the second floor and locked myself inside that I realized they had all been taken, as if they had vanished into nothing while we ran for safety.

I panted with my soft cock out on the other side of the door, but suddenly everything was silent. Nothing was loud or breaking or burning.

When I looked behind me, a large bed sat covered with a dusty sheet. It couldn't be.

Pulling open the door, I saw the cobwebs first, hanging in the darkness. I didn't understand how I had gotten there, but I was in the other house. The one close to Beachside. And everyone was gone.

I called into the dimness of the hallway, "Hello?" and my own voice echoed back. At the end, as it had hung before, was the portrait. Walking slowly, I could see even from halfway down the sheet-covered stretch that something had changed. The young man who had been on his knees was older and in the standing position. I knew why he looked familiar now. And next to him, kneeling, was me.

Leaning in close, I surveyed the image of the men in a way I hadn't been able to before. I traced the deep colors of the faces and details. It seemed to have captured every hair and my body and Usher's eyes, those piercing yet kind eyes, were just as I remembered them.

I'd been naked up until that point, still full of cum from hours of being edged, and knew it was almost out of my control when I began pumping at my cock. Looking deep into Usher's face, the way his body filled the fancy suit he always wore, it took no time at all for my load to spill onto the lush carpet below. I closed my eyes tightly as I came; something had finally released.

When I opened them again, the portrait had changed once more. Instead of two men, there was only one. The Usher I knew was gone, and in his place was the boy from the previous painting. Me, in the fancy suit. There was a nameplate I hadn't noticed before, below the image, and although the man had never asked, if he had, I would have told him my name was Madden.

It was what the small silver plaque said until I looked down to see the imitation was now manifesting in reality. I felt warm and layered. Every part of my hairy body was dressed from head-to-toe in fabric that rubbed against me in a way that felt expensive. The chandeliers and sconces clicked on in the mansion and classical music, like the violin I'd watched the boy in the jockstrap play, cascaded from the linked speakers. All the cobwebs and sheets were gone. Everything inside sparkled.

Looking back at the plaque, my name melted away and replaced itself with five letters spelling out: U-s-h-e-r.

"What do I have to do?" I asked the house, but it said nothing in return. Once again, I was alone in a place not far from water people called the ocean, but never the sea. But as I clicked my shiny shoes through the marble surfaces of what seemed to be my new home, I couldn't shake the feeling that in a world where I had always been the colorful shell creature seeking shelter, the House of Otter had other ideas of who it needed me to become.

The End

LEO SPARX

L eo Sparx is a digital artist who is bringing his fascination with the history of queer sex to the literary erotica world. Inspiration for his work is often found during virtual orgies, trips to offbeat museums, or classic—occasionally spooky—literature. His unique blend of steamy sensations and dark passion takes the reader on a kinky exploration and allows them to experience encounters in unexpected locations.

www.leosparx.com

instagram.com/authorleosparx

twitter.com/authorleosparx

authorleosparx@gmail.com

MORE LEO SPARX BOOKS
Before Alexander
Claiming Alexander
Taming Alexander
Saving Alexander
The Case of Armando
Unwrap Me: An XXX-mas Anthology

LGBT

Beau Lake

(Paranormal Romance)

The Best Beside Me

The Beast Within Me

Taming the Beast: a Novella

The Beast After Me

Dominic N. Ashen

(Fantasy Erotica)

Steel & Thunder

Storms & Sacrifice

Grayson Ace

(erotica)

How I Got Here

First Year Out of th Closet

You're Only a Top?

You're Only a Bottom?

I Think I'm a Serial Swiper

V.C.Willis

(Fantasy Romance)

The Prince's Priest

The Priest's Assassin

Erotica
Honey Cummings
Sleeping with Sasquatch
Cuddling with Chupacabra
Naked with New Jersey Devil
Laying with the Lady in Blue
Wanton Woman in White
Beating it with Bloody Mary

Beau and Professor Bestialora
The Goat's Gruff
Goldie and Her Three Beards
Pied Piper's Pipe
Princess Pea's Bed
Pinocchio and the Blow Up Doll
Jack's Beanstalk

www.ingramcontent.com/pod-product-compliance
Lightning Source LLC
Chambersburg PA
CBHW020345110726
47898CB00003B/1047